The Hope of Spring

A Lancaster County Saga

The Hope of Spring

WANDA E. BRUNSTETTER

Print ISBN 978-1-62029-144-3

eBook Editions:
Adobe Digital Edition (.epub) 978-1-62416-036-3
Kindle and MobiPocket Edition (.prc) 978-1-62416-035-6

All scripture quotations are taken from the King James Version of the Bible.

This book is a work of fiction. Names, characters, places, and incidents are either products of the author's imagination or used fictitiously. Any similarity to actual people, organizations, and/or events is purely coincidental.

Cover design: Kirk DouPonce, DogEared Design
Cover photography: Steve Gardner, PixelWorks Studios

Published by Barbour Publishing, Inc., P.O. Box 719, Uhrichsville, Ohio 44683, www.barbourbooks.com

Our mission is to publish and distribute inspirational products offering exceptional value and biblical encouragement to the masses.

Printed in the United States of America.

Bear ye one another's burdens,
and so fulfil the law of Christ.

GALATIANS 6:2

CHAPTER 1

Ronks, Pennsylvania

"There's no need for you to fuss over me," Meredith said as her mother tucked a blanket under her chin. "I'm not having any more contractions, and I don't see why I can't go home to my own house."

Mom patted Meredith's arm affectionately. "You came close to losing the *boppli* yesterday, and the doctor said you need to rest for the next several weeks until your pregnancy is no longer at risk. I'm guessing you won't do that if you go back to your house and start looking around at things you want to do. So, since you need someone to take care of you right now, and you shouldn't be doing anything strenuous, it's best if you stay here with us for the time being."

Meredith knew Mom was right, but that didn't make it any easier to deal with. She wanted to carry the baby to full term and have a homebirth in her own home in a natural way, with the midwife present.

"I'm sorry about not being able to fix supper for you and the family last night," Meredith apologized. "I was looking forward to cooking you a meal."

Mom shook her head. "Don't worry about that. There'll be plenty of other times you can make us supper. Right now, you need only be concerned about yourself and the boppli."

"I know." Meredith settled back on the sofa and tried to relax. "Did you get a chance to meet Jonah when you were at the hospital?" she asked.

"We did, but just for a few minutes, when we first got there. We're grateful he stopped by your place when he did and got the help you needed so quickly. Jonah seems like a caring young man. I'm sure he'll fit in well with our community."

"He was kind when I worked with him at

the restaurant in Pinecraft, as well."

Mom's eyebrows lifted. "Is he the same young man who wrote letters to you for a few years after you returned from Florida?"

"*Jah*." Meredith sighed. "I don't know what I would have done if he hadn't stopped by when he did. With the way I was hurting, and then having to trudge through the snow, I might not have made it to the phone shack in time to call for help."

Mom clicked her tongue. "Which is exactly why you shouldn't be alone."

Tears seeped out from under Meredith's lashes and splashed onto her cheeks. "I appreciate you letting me stay here, Mom, but you really don't need one more person to take care of right now."

"It's not a problem," Mom said, smiling at Meredith. "Around here everyone has a job to do, and right now, my job is looking after you."

"But I have responsibilities at home, and now I have a hospital bill to pay, so I really need to get busy and make some head coverings to sell. Then there's that spare room next to mine. I want to get it painted and fixed up before the boppli comes."

"Since the baby isn't due until July, there's plenty of time for that. Your *daed* can do the painting as soon as he finds the time, and Stanley will take care of your horses, get the mail, and check for phone messages after school every day." Mom gave Meredith's shoulder a gentle squeeze. "Your daed is over at your place right now, checking on things. I believe he was planning to fix the piece of siding that broke off your house."

"I should have told Dad to get the sloppy joes, potato salad, and macaroni salad out of my refrigerator and bring everything back here so we could have them for supper. That way, you won't have to cook anything tonight."

"That's okay. We can get your *bruder* to go after the food if your daed doesn't think of it. Now I want you to relax and quit worrying about things."

In hindsight, Meredith knew she should have taken better care and not done anything too strenuous yesterday. It had been foolish to carry the ladder from the barn up to the second-floor bedroom. Now her body needed time to rest and heal. She really had no choice but to stay here right now, so she may as well try to relax and enjoy the pampering.

I've lost Luke, Meredith thought as her eyes drifted shut, *and I won't take the chance of losing our baby.*

Bird-in-Hand, Pennsylvania

Jonah had just finished working at the buggy shop for the day, so he decided to go over to Meredith's house. She was supposed to get out of the hospital this afternoon, and he wanted to see how she was doing.

Jonah borrowed his dad's horse and buggy, but he couldn't seem to get the horse, Knickers, to move along very fast. No matter where he went with the horse and buggy, Jonah usually enjoyed taking in the scenery, but not today. He barely noticed the snow in the fields, and the blue jays squawking overhead seemed more of an annoyance to him.

Finally, he was there, and after securing Knickers to the hitching rail near the barn, he headed for the house. Jonah had just stepped onto the porch, when another horse and buggy pulled into the yard. After the driver got out and secured the horse, Jonah realized it was Meredith's dad, whom he'd met at the hospital. Jonah waved and waited for Philip to join him on the porch.

"If you're lookin' for Meredith, she's not here," Philip said.

"Is she still in the hospital?" Jonah asked.

"Nope. She was released this afternoon, and she'll be staying at our place for a while."

Jonah nodded. "Guess that makes sense. It's probably not a good idea for her to be here alone, trying to do things by herself."

"It sure isn't—especially now that she's expecting a boppli. Losing Luke has been hard on Meredith. She loved him a lot. But having a baby will help keep his memory alive." Philip leaned against the porch railing. "It'll be hard for her to raise the baby alone, so we're gonna help out as much as we can, despite her objections."

"Will Meredith sell her house and move in with you permanently?" Jonah questioned.

Philip shrugged. "I'm not sure about that. My daughter can be stubborn sometimes, and I know she wants to make it on her own. But there are bills and taxes to pay, and with no money comin' in, she may be forced to sell."

"That'd be a shame," Jonah said, wishing there was something he could do to help out. "Won't some folks in this community give Meredith money?"

"There will probably be a benefit auction to help with her medical expenses." Philip glanced toward the barn. "But I'm thinkin' she ought to sell Luke's horse, because she doesn't need him anymore, and I'm sure the gelding would go for a fairly good price."

"I'd be interested in buying it," Jonah said. "The horse I had in Ohio was getting old, so I sold him before I moved here, and now I need a new one."

Philip reached under his hat and scratched his head. "That should work out well for Meredith, but I'll have to discuss it with her first, of course."

"Since she's staying over at your place, why don't I follow you home? Then I can ask her about buying Luke's horse."

Philip shook his head. "I think it's better if I talk to her first. Why don't you drop by our place sometime tomorrow?"

"All right then, I'll come over after work

tomorrow afternoon," Jonah agreed, although he was disappointed he wouldn't be seeing Meredith until then.

Out back, an energetic German shorthair pointer barked frantically from his kennel. "Guess I'd better get ole Fritzy boy and take him home with me," Philip said. "Poor mutt probably can't figure out what's goin' on. Luke is gone, and now the dog's most likely wondering where Meredith is."

Jonah extended his hand. "It was nice to see you again, Philip. I'll take a look at the horse before I go so I'll have a better idea of how much I should offer for him."

Ronks

Meredith had been resting on the sofa most of the day and was bored. Lying here gave her too much time to think about Luke and how much she missed him. Her mind drifted back to the day they'd said goodbye and the sincere expression she'd seen on his face. If she had known it would be the last time she'd ever see her beloved husband, she would have said so many things.

Tears welled in Meredith's eyes and trickled down her cheeks. *Oh, Luke, I love you so much.* The thought that she would never see his handsome, smiling face again was almost too much to comprehend.

Forcing herself to think about something else, Meredith began to fret because she couldn't be at home doing the things she'd planned in preparation for the baby. If only there was something she could do while she rested—anything that would keep her mind off the troubles she faced and help her focus on something else. She'd always been the type to keep her hands busy, and doing nothing was so frustrating.

"Would you like a cup of tea?" Meredith's grandmother asked as she entered the living room with a tray in her hands.

Meredith nodded appreciatively. "That'd be nice."

Grandma Smucker set the tray on the coffee table, poured each of them a cup of tea, and took a seat in the rocker across from Meredith. "How are you feeling, dear one?"

Meredith managed a weak smile. "Better

than yesterday. I overdid it, and because of my stupidity, I almost lost the boppli."

Grandma slowly shook her head. "Don't be so hard on yourself, Meredith. We all make mistakes."

"I guess I'm full of *hochmut*, or I would have asked for help painting the baby's room."

"You should never be too proud to ask. That's what families are for, you know." Grandma took a sip of tea and winked at Meredith. "You're a lot like me, though. It was hard to move in with your folks after your grandpa died, and I still feel bad about them having to support me. But I know they're doing it because they love me, and for that, I'm grateful." She sighed as she set her cup on the coffee table. "It's sad to say, but some folks, like Alma Beechy, don't have any family around to help."

"I appreciate my family and friends," Meredith said, taking a sip of tea and savoring the delicious flavor of ginger, which soothed her upset stomach almost immediately. "My friend Dorine Yoder suggested that I make head coverings to sell. I was planning to start doing that right away, but now I guess it'll have to wait awhile."

"I've made a few coverings in my day," Grandma said, "so I'd be happy to help when you're feeling up to doing some sewing."

"*Danki*, I would like that."

"How are you doing?" Dad asked as he and Mom entered the room.

"I'm okay. Just tired of lying around doing nothing but worrying about things—including my finances," she answered honestly.

"First things, first. I have a surprise for you." Dad grinned at Meredith and went out to the back porch. When he returned, he had Fritz. The dog spied Meredith and raced over to her, resting his head gently on her lap as though sensing that he needed to take it easy with her. His stub of a tail, however, flopped back and forth on the floor, beating a rhythm of happiness. Meredith laughed at how funny he looked. It felt good to find something to laugh about.

"Hey, pup," she said, patting the top of his head. "How are you doin', boy?"

Fritz slurped Meredith's hand in response.

"I bet you were lonely last night, weren't you, pup? I'm sorry I had to leave you alone in your kennel all night." Meredith felt her nerves begin to relax as she continued to pet Fritz, and he alternated between licking and nuzzling her hand.

"I think I may have an answer that could help you. At least, it will help out with your finances," Dad said.

"Oh, what's that?" Meredith asked as she pampered Fritz with soothing murmurs.

"I ran into Jonah Miller at your place today, and he's interested in buying Luke's *gaul*."

"What was Jonah doing at my house, and why does he need a horse? Doesn't he have one of his own?" Meredith questioned.

"He went over there to check on you. And jah, he did have a horse when he was in Ohio, but he sold it before he moved here, so he needs a new one. Said his other horse was gettin' too old."

Mom's eyebrows pulled tightly together. "I wish we were better off financially so we could buy the horse."

"First off, we don't need another horse, and second, I don't need the reminder of how bad off we are financially." Dad rubbed the side of his slightly crooked nose and frowned. "When you say things like that, Luann, it makes me feel like a failure—like I can't provide well enough for our family."

Mom shook her head. "I didn't mean that at all, Philip. I know how hard you work to keep your stands at three farmers' markets going, and I hope you're not thinking of taking on any more."

"I had given it some consideration," he said. "Thought maybe I could get a stand going at the Crossroads Farmers' Market in Gratz."

"But that's clear up in Dauphin County." Mom planted both hands on her hips and looked at him with a determined expression. "Besides the expense of hiring a driver to take you there every week, it would mean you'd be gone from home even more than you are already."

"I don't like being away from the family, either," he said with a slow shake of his head, "but I need to make sure we have enough money coming in to provide for everyone's needs."

Mom clenched her teeth. "I'm sorry I even mentioned our financial situation. Please, Philip, let's pray about this before you decide to take on another stand."

"Yep. I'll definitely be doin' that. In the meantime, though," he said, looking back at

Meredith, "what do you think about sellin' Luke's gaul?"

She swallowed hard as tears pricked the backs of her eyes. If she sold Luke's horse, she'd be letting go of something that had been important to him. But if she kept the gelding, she'd never use him for pulling the buggy because Socks was too spirited for her to handle.

"It would be hard to let the horse go, knowing how much Luke liked him," Meredith said. "Can I think about it for a day or two before I give Jonah an answer?"

Dad nodded. "Sure, take all the time you need. In the meantime, though, I also brought something else back with me."

"More surprises, Dad?" Meredith asked.

"Not exactly. I saw a bag of hamburger rolls on your kitchen table, so I took a peek in the refrigerator and spotted two delicious-looking salads and some ground beef you'd browned for sloppy joes. Figured we may as well eat it here tonight so it won't go to waste." Dad grinned and thumped his stomach. "So now it'll go to my waist instead."

"I'm glad you thought to look in the

refrigerator. Now Mom won't have to do much cooking for supper tonight." Meredith looked at her mother. "The ground beef has sautéed peppers and onions mixed in, and the only thing you'll have to do is add a little brown sugar, salt, pepper, a bit of mustard, and some mild chili sauce if you have some."

"I'll get that simmering right away," Mom said. "It'll be a nice treat having an evening off from cooking a big meal."

Meredith wished she could have had her family to her house for supper, but this was the next best thing. At least they could all be together, and she thanked the Lord one more time for her caring family, and most of all, that she hadn't lost the baby.

CHAPTER 2

Philadelphia, Pennsylvania

"I sure wish all this snow would go away. I'm more than ready for spring," Nurse Susan Bailey said to her sister, Anne, as they rode in Anne's compact car out of the city toward their grandparents' house in Darby.

"I wholeheartedly agree," Anne said, turning her blinker on to move to another lane. "The sooner the weather warms up, the sooner I can start jogging in the park again."

Susan smiled. Her thirty-year-old sister had always liked to be outdoors and enjoyed exercising, which was probably why she was so fit and trim. Of course, Susan had never had a problem with her weight either, but she wasn't into exercise. She figured she got enough of a workout on the job, although so did Anne, since she was a physical therapist. Anne might be extra motivated to stay in tip-top shape, so she'd be able to perform her duties without injuring herself and would be a good role model to her patients, who often needed encouragement.

Today had been one of those rare occasions when Susan's and Anne's work schedules coincided, and they'd been able to ride to and from the hospital together. The drive to work was only about ten minutes, but it was still nice to have someone to chat with along the route.

"Just think, spring's less than a month away, so we don't have too much longer to wait," Anne said, breaking into Susan's thoughts.

"I know, and as soon as the weather warms up, I'll be sticking my hands in the dirt and helping Grandpa putter around in his garden."

"You definitely inherited your desire to work in the garden from him." Anne flipped a curly tendril away from her face. "I'd rather read a good book than play in the dirt."

"I like to read, too," Susan agreed, "but not as much in the warmer weather, since I can do other things. You know how it is with me." She held up her hands. "I like to see results from something I've worked on with my hands—especially if it takes me outside."

Susan's thoughts drifted as she glanced at her polished fingernails and thought about the vegetables she and Grandpa would plant this year. Her nails wouldn't look this good once she started working the soil for their garden, but that was okay. She'd rather have dirt under her nails than give up something that brought her so much pleasure and satisfaction. Susan could almost smell the earthy aroma of the damp soil as she worked it through her fingers. Better yet, she could just about taste those delicious BLTs they would make with the juicy beefsteak tomatoes they'd pick. What wasn't there to like about biting into a sandwich made with fresh, homegrown tomatoes? Even better was sharing a meal at the picnic table Grandma and Grandpa had in the corner of their backyard, under the shade of the maple tree.

They rode in silence for a while, until they passed a homeless man holding up a sign saying he was out of work and needed money. Seeing him made Susan think about one of her patients who'd been admitted to ICU a little over a month ago. Anne must have been thinking of him, too, because she glanced over at Susan and said, "How's that John Doe of yours doing?"

"About the same. The poor guy had surgery to repair the damage that had been done to his spleen, but unfortunately he's still in a coma."

"That's too bad. Has there been any sign of him waking up?"

Susan shook her head. "He flutters his eyes and jerks his hands once in a while, but he hasn't responded to any verbal stimulation. Along with the trauma to his spleen and his vocal cords, he suffered a serious injury to his brain tissue, which resulted in a blood clot. The doctor's still giving him medicine to dissolve the clot. His other injuries included several broken ribs, a cracked sternum, and a fractured collar bone. They're healing okay on their own and won't require surgery, but I fear he may never wake up. And if he does, he may not be as he once was. We still don't know his name, so I call him Eddie." She sighed. "Even though I know he might not hear me, I talk to him about all sorts of things, and I also pray for him—sometimes out loud."

"It's good that you're doing that," Anne

said. "Doctors always encourage nurses to talk to their patients, even though they don't seem to hear what you're saying. That will keep his brain stimulated, just hearing your voice. And of course," she added, "prayer is important, too."

Susan smiled. "Well, if Eddie does hear what I'm saying, he probably thinks I'm a bit of a motormouth."

"I doubt it. Your positive attitude and compassion are the best medicine that young man can get right now." Anne switched lanes again. "I'm happy to say that most of my patients aren't in as bad a shape as your Eddie. It's easier to work with them when they're conscious and able to communicate. Hopefully, by the time Eddie is stable enough to be moved to rehab, he'll have woken up from his coma."

Bird-in-Hand

"How long will it be till supper?" Jonah asked when he entered the kitchen and found his mother in front of the sink, peeling potatoes.

She turned and smiled, her green eyes

twinkling. "You're home early today, and since I'm just getting started on the potatoes and carrots that will go with the roast we're having for supper, it won't be ready for at least another hour yet."

"Can you keep something warm for me in case I don't make it back before then?" Jonah asked as Mom handed him a piece of raw potato.

He went to the table and sprinkled a little salt on the potato before popping it into his mouth.

Mom grinned. "I see you still like eating raw potatoes."

"Some things never change," Jonah answered, enjoying the uncooked morsel. "I'll take another chunk if you don't mind."

"So, where are you going?" Mom asked, handing him one more piece.

"Over to the Kings' place to speak with Meredith. Remember, I told you last night that I planned to go over there after Dad and I finished up at the buggy shop today. I want to see about buying her husband's gaul."

Mom thumped the side of her head, pushing her covering slightly askew, and exposing the light brown bun at the back of her head. "I'd forgotten about that," she said, readjusting the covering. "I assume you'll be taking your daed's horse and buggy?"

"Yep, that's right."

"You're welcome to ride over to the Kings' on my scooter." Mom grinned, reminding Jonah of a young schoolgirl. Truth was, his fifty-six-year-old mother was so thin and petite she could almost pass for a teenage girl if it weren't for the few wrinkles on her forehead. Dad often teased her, saying she was his child-bride.

"Think I'll stick to Dad's horse and buggy," Jonah replied with a chuckle. "It'll take me less time, and won't be as hard on my legs as a scooter."

"That's true," Mom agreed, "but at least with my scooter you won't have an unruly horse to deal with on the road." She looked past Jonah toward the door. "Where's your daed?"

"Out in the barn. Said to tell you he'll be in soon." Jonah stepped up to Mom and gave her a hug. "I'm going to wash up and change into some clean clothes, then I'll be heading over to see Meredith." He snatched a raw carrot before heading out of the room, and smiled when he heard Mom crunch one, too.

Ronks

Meredith had been resting on the sofa most of the afternoon, and her youngest siblings, Owen and Katie, were getting on her nerves. They were either fussing at each other or running through the house, hollering at the top of their lungs. Owen, who'd turned three last November, had started walking by the time he was ten months old and never had any trouble keeping up with six-year-old Katie. Mom had been trying to keep the little ones quiet today, but every time she got them interested in doing something in another room, they'd end up back in the living room. With Meredith's teenage sisters, Laurie and Kendra, both working at the farmers' market today, and thirteen-year-old Nina visiting a friend after school, Mom was short-handed this evening.

"You'd better give me that!" Katie shouted as she raced past Meredith, chasing after Owen, who had taken her doll.

Meredith grimaced. *I wonder if I'll feel this*

way when my own baby is born and starts fussing or being too loud. I hope not, because I don't want to be an impatient mother.

Meredith loved her family, but she wished she could go back to the quiet of her own house. She didn't remember that the antics of her younger brothers and sisters bothered her before she got married like they did now. Maybe that was because, for over a year, it had just been her, Luke, and Fritz, with no energetic little ones underfoot.

Adding to Meredith's frustration were all the things she wanted to get done at home, and the preparations she wanted to make for the baby. But there was nothing more important than the safety of her unborn child, and most of her aggravation was from not doing anything except lying around. Hopefully, she could get started on making those head coverings soon.

She glanced around the room. Not much had changed in the large home where her family lived. From the looks of the furniture, one would never know that seven children were still being raised in this house. Most of the pieces were still original and had been here when

Meredith was growing up. Mom had a knack for taking good care of things and teaching her children to do the same. With a little sanding and some varnish, Mom had brought new life to some of the old pieces of furniture she and Dad had purchased at auctions a long time ago. Meredith had been told that some of the pieces in this room had been handed down to Mom and Dad from their parents. She remembered Dad saying once, "If you take care of what you have, it'll last a long time."

Looking around, the proof was here, right down to the large oak table and chairs in the dining room. A lot of celebrations had been held around that table, and many great memories were made with family and friends.

I hope I can be a good role model for my child, like my parents still are with all of us, Meredith thought. She closed her eyes, breathing in the wonderful aromas coming from the kitchen. Was that fried chicken she smelled? She hoped so. Mom's fried chicken was the best.

"I'm sorry if the little ones are disturbing you," Mom said, dashing into the living room, hoisting Owen onto her hip, and taking hold of Katie's hand. "Your grandma and I have been busy fixing supper, and we figured either Stanley or Arlene would keep an eye on the little ones, but things didn't quite go as planned."

"Where are my little bruder *un schweschder*?" Meredith asked.

"Stanley's in the barn doing some chores, and Arlene's resting upstairs in her room. She came home from school this afternoon complaining of a *koppweh*."

Meredith sighed. "Arlene's not the only one with a headache. My head's pounding so hard I can barely think."

"Why don't you go to your room and lie down?" Mom suggested. "I'll call you when supper's ready."

"Maybe I will." Meredith swung her legs over the side of the sofa, and had just started across the room when a knock sounded on the door. "I'll get that," she said, looking at Mom. "You've got your hands full right now."

Mom nodded and hurried into the kitchen, with the two little ones in tow.

When Meredith opened the front door, she was surprised to see Jonah Miller.

"*Wie geht's?*" he asked with a smile.

"I'm doing okay," Meredith replied, making

no mention of her headache. "Come in out of the cold," she said, opening the door wider.

"Danki."

When Jonah stepped in, Meredith motioned for him to take a seat in the rocker, and she returned to the sofa.

"I want to thank you for calling 911 for me." Meredith looked at Jonah, feeling shy all of a sudden. "Your timing was perfect."

"You're welcome, and I'd have to say that it was God's timing, not mine, that brought me to your house. I'm glad you're doing better and were able to come here to stay with your folks." Jonah removed his straw hat and raked his fingers through the ends of his dark, curly hair. "Uh. . .the reason I'm here is to talk to you about your husband's gaul."

She nodded. "My daed said you were interested in buying the horse, but there's something you need to know."

"What's that?"

"Socks can be a bit spirited, so he may not be what you need. Luke seemed to be the only one who could handle the horse effectively."

Jonah smiled. "I've had spirited horses before, so I'm not worried about that."

Meredith sucked in her lower lip as she mulled things over. Jonah was probably right about handling Luke's horse. It was just the thought of giving Socks up that made her feel like crying. Unfortunately, it was another reminder that the love of her life was gone and would never be back.

At least she had warned Jonah about Socks being feisty. The rest would be in Jonah's hands if he ended up buying the horse. "How much would you be willing to pay for the horse?" Meredith questioned.

"Does two thousand dollars sound okay?"

"Oh, no," Meredith said with a shake of her head. "That's way too much money."

Jonah leaned forward, looking at Meredith with a most sincere expression. "I checked the horse over before I left your place yesterday, and I think Socks is worth every bit of that."

Meredith sat for several seconds, then finally nodded. She needed the money. She just wished she didn't have to part with Luke's horse. If only he hadn't been killed on that bus. If he'd just stayed home like she'd wanted him to do, instead of heading for Indiana to buy his uncle's business. Would she ever stop regretting that she hadn't tried harder to convince Luke not to go?

Oh, Luke, she thought, fighting back tears, *I don't think I'll ever get over losing you.*

CHAPTER 3

As Meredith headed down the hall from her room, she yawned and stretched her arms over her head. It was the second Monday of March, and she was more than ready to go home. Not only were her younger siblings still getting on her nerves, but she missed her own surroundings and the things that reminded her of Luke. She was feeling stronger, with no more contractions, so she didn't see any reason to keep staying with her folks. Now she just needed to convince Mom of that.

When Meredith entered the kitchen, she found Mom in front of the stove, stirring a kettle of oatmeal. "*Guder mariye,*" Meredith said, moving across the room.

Mom turned and smiled. "Good morning. Besides me, you're the first one up. Did you sleep well last night?"

Meredith shook her head. "Not really. Between Dad's snoring, the wind howling and rattling my bedroom window, and then Owen crying out several times during the night, I had a hard time staying asleep."

"I'm sorry about that," Mom apologized. "I've grown used to your daed's snoring, so it doesn't bother me that much, but I'll ask him to be sure he wears one of those nose strips he bought awhile ago. And I think things will be better with Owen once he gets over his cold." Mom sighed. "I'm not sure about the window, though. The March winds are picking up, and for as long as I can remember, that window's been making a racket. I'll ask your daed to look at it. Maybe there's something he can do to make the window tighter so it won't rattle so much."

"You don't have to worry about any of those things, because I'm ready to go home," Meredith blurted out. "It's quieter there, and since I'm feeling better now, I'm sure I can manage fine on my own."

Mom's lips pursed. "It's not a good idea for you to be alone, Meredith. I shudder to think what would have happened if Jonah Miller hadn't dropped by to see you the day you started having contractions."

"I'm glad he was there, but if I had been alone when the pains got bad, I would have somehow made my way out to the phone shack and called for help," Meredith said in her own defense. She could see by the look on Mom's face that she wasn't convinced. Truthfully, Meredith knew she might not have made it, and she was thankful that Jonah had showed up when he did.

"If it's too noisy for you here, then we can talk to Luke's folks and see if you can stay with them, like you did for a few weeks after Luke died."

"Sadie and Elam are getting up in years, and they don't need me to look after."

"I'm sure it wouldn't be an imposition. They'd probably love having you there for a while again."

Meredith shook her head. "I don't need to stay with anyone, Mom."

"What if someone stays with you at your

house? Would you be okay with that?"

"Who?"

"I was thinking of your sister Laurie. I'm almost sure she'd be willing, and I know she would be a big help to you."

"But Laurie has her stand at the farmers' market, so she'd be gone most of the day," Meredith pointed out. "How would that help me?"

"But the market's only open on Fridays and Saturdays through April. And in May, it's just three days a week. It's not until July that it goes to four. On the days Laurie's working, we can ask someone else to come and stay with you." Mom's eyes brightened, and she snapped her fingers. "I know. We can see if Alma Beechy would go to your house whenever Laurie's at the market."

Meredith's jaw clenched. She didn't want anyone babysitting her, but if she didn't agree, Mom would insist that she stay with the family.

"Okay," she said with a slow nod. "If Laurie's agreeable, then she can move in with me for now, and if Alma's willing, she can come during the hours Laurie's not there."

Mom's face relaxed a bit, and she gave

Meredith a hug. "I know you think it's not necessary, but it'll make me feel a little more at ease." She patted Meredith's growing stomach. "It's nice to see that you're starting to show. It makes me even more excited about becoming a *groossmudder*."

"I'm excited about being a *mudder*, too," Meredith said.

"Just wait until your child is born," Mom added. "No matter what age he or she should be, you'll still worry, same as I do now."

Mom was right. Even though she was only four-and-a-half months pregnant, Meredith already worried about her baby.

Darby, Pennsylvania

"Would you please pass the syrup?" Susan's grandfather asked after she'd handed him the platter of fresh buttermilk pancakes Grandma had made for breakfast.

Susan smiled, and after she'd passed him the maple syrup, she bit into one of the pancakes on her plate and wiped the sticky, warm syrup from her lips. "Yum! Grandma, this is delicious. You're such a good cook."

Grandma laughed, her cheeks turning pink. "You say that at nearly every one of our meals."

"That's because it's true," Anne agreed from her place across the table. "I doubt that I'll ever be able to fix a meal as tasty as any of yours."

Grandpa leaned over and kissed Grandma's cheek. "Now you know why I've stayed married to her all these years."

Grandma playfully swatted his arm. "Oh, Henry, you're such a big tease."

Susan smiled. She loved watching the camaraderie between her grandparents and felt blessed to have them both in her life. Many people didn't have a close relationship with their grandparents, and some didn't know them at all. Susan couldn't imagine that, and it made her all the more thankful for what she and Anne had.

"Not to change the subject or anything," Anne said, "but Susan, I was wondering if you're still interested in reading that Amish novel I told you about."

Susan nodded. "Yes, I sure am."

"Great. I'll get it from my room as soon as we're done with breakfast."

"The Amish are quite an unusual group of people," Grandpa said. "I admire their commitment to keeping true to their heritage."

"Yes," Grandma agreed. "Unfortunately, for many people, there isn't much commitment to anything in this day and age, and if there is, it seems to be short-lived."

"Speaking of the Amish," Anne said, "I still want to visit Lancaster soon, to look around some of the shops where they sell Amish-made products."

"Are you looking for anything in particular?" Grandma asked, finishing the last bite of her pancake as she took her plate to the sink.

Anne shook her head. "I think I'll know it when I see it, though." She looked over at Susan and grinned. "As soon as we both know our work schedules for April, let's plan a day when we can go to Lancaster like we talked about doing before."

"I suppose we could," Susan agreed. "It would be something different to do, at least."

Grandma nodded, testing the water in her sink before starting the dishes. "As hard as you two work, you deserve to do something fun on your day off."

"Maybe you and Grandpa would like to go, too," Anne suggested.

Grandma looked at Grandpa. "What do you think about that, Henry?"

He shrugged his shoulders. "I don't know, Norma. Guess we'll just have to wait and see how it goes."

Bird-in-Hand

"Where are you headed, Son?" Jonah's mother asked when he slipped into his jacket and put his straw hat on his head.

"Since today's my day off, I plan to run a few errands, and I thought it'd be good to take my new gaul out for a run," he answered, stopping near the back door. "In case you're wondering, I should be home in plenty of time to help with the chores before supper."

Dad looked up from reading the newspaper and frowned. "I still can't figure out why you bought that gelding. The horse is too spirited, if you ask me."

Jonah bobbed his head. "You're right about

that. Meredith warned me about his friskiness before I bought him. But I think with some work and a little time, Socks will settle down and be a good horse for me."

"I've seen the way he acts around our *hund*," Mom said, "and I don't like it one little bit. Why, the other day when Socks was waiting at the hitching rail, he nearly kicked poor Herbie in the head."

"That's probably because the dog was pestering him," Jonah said.

Mom shook her head vigorously. "Herbie's an easygoing animal, and it's not like him to bother any of our livestock. I think that new horse is just plain mean." Her eyebrows furrowed. "I'll bet the March winds we've been having will spook that critter of yours, too."

Jonah didn't argue. He figured there was no point. Once Mom made up her mind about something, it practically took a miracle to change it. Well, maybe after Socks became adjusted to his new surroundings, he'd prove to Mom that she was wrong.

"Speaking of Herbie, I've been wondering where he came from," Jonah said, wanting to change the subject.

"Guess you could say that Herbie found us," Dad replied. "A few weeks before you moved here, the dog showed up on our doorstep, and he's been with us ever since." He went on to explain how he'd posted Dog Found signs all over the community, on telephone poles, and in local grocery stores, as well as passing the word to folks when they came into his buggy shop. Since no one knew about any lost dog or who the border collie belonged to, as time went by, Herbie became one of the family.

"Ah, I see. And how'd you come up with his name?" Jonah inquired.

"That's another thing that just seemed to happen," Mom said. "When Herbie first showed up, we started saying 'here boy' whenever we took food out to him or when we didn't know where he was. Then when it looked like the dog was here to stay, I decided to give him a name."

"We never kept him tied or penned up, thinking that one day he might try to find his way home," Dad put in, "but he seemed to like it here, and since he always responded to 'here boy,' your *mamm* came up with the name 'Herbie,' since it sort of sounded like 'here boy.'" He chuckled. "Herbie seemed to like it, too, so that's how the name stuck."

"When we're with him, Herbie watches, like he's waiting for us to tell him to do something." Mom glanced out the kitchen window, where Herbie lay in front of the buggy shop. "Just look at him out there. I'll bet he's waiting for someone to show up."

"That's right," Dad agreed. "And the dog always lets us know when someone's coming by giving a few loud barks." He grinned. "Herbie's friendly with most people, though. Whenever I'm in the shop and a customer comes in, Herbie greets them with a wag of his tail, and does he ever like the attention when someone stops to pet him."

"It sounds like Herbie's found himself a good home," Jonah said.

"Jah, and we're glad he's here with us. Oh, by the way, Jonah, where all are you going today?" Mom asked as Jonah's hand touched the doorknob.

"For one thing, I'll be stopping by the Shoe and Boot store," Jonah replied. He wished he didn't have to answer to Mom; it made him feel like a schoolboy.

"That shouldn't take all day," she said. "Are

there some other places you'll be stopping, as well?"

"Stop badgering the boy, Sarah," Dad said, flapping the end of his newspaper at Mom. "It shouldn't matter where he's going."

Mom's lips compressed. "I wasn't badgering him, Raymond. Just was curious to know why he said he'd be home in time for the evening chores." Mom glanced at the clock on the far wall, and then at Jonah. "It's not even noon yet, and if you're just going to the Shoe and Boot store, I wouldn't think you'd be gone more than a few hours at the most."

Jonah tapped his foot impatiently. This inquisition was getting worse. "If you must know, I'm planning to stop by the Kings' place to see how Meredith is doing."

Deep wrinkles formed across Mom's forehead. "Do you think that's a good idea?"

"Why wouldn't it be?" Jonah asked. He had an inkling of what she was going to say next but hoped she wouldn't.

"Well, some folks might get the wrong idea."

"The wrong idea about what?" Dad questioned.

"Meredith's husband hasn't even been gone

two months yet, and some might think our son has taken an interest in her." Mom tapped her fingers along the edge of the table. "That's not the case, is it, Jonah?"

" 'Course not," Jonah was quick to say. "Meredith is just a good friend, and I'm doing what the Bible says in Galatians 6:2: 'Bear ye one another's burdens, and so fulfil the law of Christ.' "

"I know what the Bible says." Mom flapped her hand. "But Meredith is the friend you had an interest in after you came back from Sarasota with stars in your eyes."

"Well, you two enjoy your day," Jonah said, giving no reply to Mom's last comment. "Looks like we might get some rain," he called over his shoulder as he headed out the door, needing to sidestep this conversation. He wasn't about to say anything more, but deep down, he hoped that someday, after Meredith had recovered from her husband's death, she might take an interest in him.

CHAPTER 4

Stepping onto the porch, Jonah realized it was raining. That was pretty typical for this time of the year, and it was a lot better than snow, but he really preferred sunshine to rain. He looked forward to nicer weather so he could get out Mom and Dad's grill and cook some steaks, burgers, or chicken. He was sure Mom would appreciate not having to cook once he started grilling, too.

By the time Jonah got his buggy out of the barn and Socks hitched to it, he was pretty wet. He grabbed the towel he kept on the floor of the backseat for such occasions, lifted his straw hat, and wiped his face and head. Hopefully the rain would let up soon, or he'd probably be drenched by the time he finished running all his errands.

Socks bulked a bit when Jonah tried to back him away from the hitching rail, but once he got the horse turned and headed down the driveway, things went okay. Socks liked to trot at a fairly good pace, so Jonah had to keep a firm grip on the reins. If he gave the horse too much slack, he'd take off like a shot. And on a busy stretch of road such as this, that would not be a good thing.

Jonah's first stop was at the Shoe and Boot store, where Seth Yoder helped him find a good pair of work boots. As he left the store, a strong wind nearly blew his hat off. At least it had stopped raining. He glanced at the sky, still heavy with gray clouds. Now if only the wind would quit sending chills down the back of his neck.

Socks pawed at the ground, while chewing on the hitching rail. Talk about an impatient animal! "You can relax now, Socks," Jonah said soothingly as he released the horse's lines from the rail. "We'll soon be on our way again."

As they traveled down the road toward the

Kings' place, Socks started tossing his head from side to side, especially when a gust of wind blew clusters of old wet leaves across the road in front of them. A couple of times the horse acted like he was going to rear up, but Jonah quickly brought him under control. As they neared the furniture store where Meredith's husband used to work, Socks bolted right into the parking lot, nearly running into the fence along the side of the road. Was this overly zealous horse looking for his master? Jonah wondered. Did Socks miss his previous owner? Could that be why he was acting up? Of course, it didn't help that the roads were still wet, but Jonah had a feeling there was more to it than that. Socks might be a one-man horse; however Jonah had always had a way with horses, and he was determined to win this one over.

"Easy now," he said, turning the horse back onto the road. "Your master's not here anymore. I'm your new owner."

A car whizzed by, and Socks whinnied. "It's okay, boy," Jonah called. "There's nothing to worry about."

As soon as Jonah spoke, he realized his words weren't exactly true. Horse and buggies were vulnerable on the roads. As a buggy maker, he knew all too well how devastating an accident could be to a buggy, its passengers, and even the horse if it was hit by a car, or worse a big truck or bus. And there were lots of tour buses in Lancaster County.

Jonah grimaced, remembering a time when a speeding pickup truck had crested a hill near the small town of Charm, Ohio, and smashed into the back of a buggy. Another time, the driver of a car in Sugarcreek swerved to avoid hitting a buggy and ended up ramming into another buggy going in the opposite direction.

Other vehicles weren't the only thing that caused buggy accidents, though. Horses sometimes spooked and ran out of control because of water splashing from passing vehicles, loud noises, or uneven roadways. Jonah had seen many buggies in such bad condition that they were beyond repair. That meant the owner had the expense of buying a new one, which could cost anywhere from two thousand to five thousand dollars.

All of Jonah's knowledge about buggy accidents made him work even harder to keep Socks under control. Finally, the Kings' house came into view, and Jonah was glad when the horse turned easily up the driveway. No doubt Socks had brought Meredith and Luke here a good many times, so he probably felt comfortable in his surroundings.

After Jonah had Socks secured at the hitching rail, he sprinted for the house. He was about to knock on the door, when it swung open, and a freckle-faced boy, who looked to be around ten or eleven years old, stepped onto the porch. "Can I help ya?" the little fellow asked.

Jonah nodded. "I'm Jonah Miller, and I'm here to see Meredith."

The boy squinted his blue eyes as he stared up at Jonah. "So you're the buggy maker's son, huh?"

"That's right, and I'm also a buggy maker."

The boy nodded. "My *naame* is Stanley."

Jonah held out his hand. "It's nice to meet you, Stanley. I'm guessing you're Meredith's little bruder."

Stanley squared his shoulders and stretched to his full height. "I ain't her *little* brother. Owen's the little one. He's three, but I'm twelve."

Jonah bit back a chuckle. "When your sister and I were teenagers, she mentioned you in one of her letters, but you were her only little bruder back then."

Stanley flicked a blob of white cat hair off his trousers and grinned. "Guess that was true enough."

"So is it okay if I come in?" Jonah asked, hoping he'd won the boy over. "I'd like to see how Meredith's doing."

Stanley shook his head. "She ain't here."

"She ain't? I mean, she's not?"

"Huh-uh. Meredith went back to her own house this mornin' 'cause the little ones were gettin' on her nerves." Stanley snickered. "Oh, and Dad's snorin' was keepin' her awake at night, too."

Jonah smiled. "So I assume if she went home that she must be feeling better?"

Stanley shrugged. "Don't know for sure, but I do know that our sister Laurie went with her, 'cause Mom said she had to."

Before Jonah could comment, Meredith's mother stuck her head through the open doorway. "Wie geht's?" she asked, smiling at Jonah.

"I'm doing fine. I came by to see how Meredith's doing, but Stanley said she went home."

"That's right, and Laurie will be staying with her most of the time. When Laurie's working at the farmers' market, Alma Beechy will be with Meredith." Deep wrinkles formed across Luann's forehead. "I'd be a nervous wreck if Meredith was home by herself right now. She came close to losing the boppli, and might have, too, if you hadn't been there to call for help." Her face relaxed some. "I believe the Lord must have sent you to my daughter's house that day."

"I think you might be right about that." Jonah shuffled his feet a few times. "Do you think Meredith would mind if I stopped over to see her right now? I want to make sure she's doing all right and see if there's anything she might need."

Luann smiled. "That's nice of you, and since you're going that way, would you mind taking something to Meredith for me? I was going to send it with her this morning, but things got hectic around here and I forgot."

"I don't mind at all. What have you got?" Jonah asked.

"A bunch of posies," Stanley spoke up, motioning to the two pots of primroses sitting on one end of the porch. "Meredith likes *blumme*."

"I'd be happy to take the flowers to her," Jonah said. "There's more than enough room in the back of my buggy."

Luann glanced across the yard. "How's Luke's horse doing for you? Has he given you any trouble?"

Jonah wasn't about to admit that Socks had acted up on the way over because he didn't want Meredith to hear about it and feel guilty for selling him the horse.

"Socks and I are still getting to know each other," he said, carefully choosing his words. "And I'm sure after a while we'll get along just fine."

Stanley frowned. "I don't like that gaul. He tried to bite me once when I was hitchin' him to the rail for Luke."

Jonah didn't like the sound of that. If Socks had been unruly even when his master was around, maybe he'd never get him trained. Well, he'd just have to keep trying.

"Stanley, why don't you help Jonah by carrying one of those pots out to his buggy?" Luann said. "Just be sure you stay away from the horse."

"Okay, Mom." The boy bent down, picked

up a pot, and tromped off across the yard.

"Is there anything else you'd like me to take Meredith?" Jonah asked as he picked up the second pot of flowers.

Luann nodded. "As a matter of fact, there is. My mamm made some of Meredith's favorite ginger *kichlin* this morning, and I'm sure she'd enjoy having some."

"No problem. I'd be happy to take the cookies to Meredith." *Is it too much to hope that Meredith might offer me a few of those cookies?* Jonah thought as his stomach rumbled.

"What would you like for lunch today?" Laurie asked Meredith as they sat on the sofa in the living room, drinking hot chocolate while they visited.

Meredith shrugged. "It really doesn't matter. But you don't have to wait on me, because I can fix my own lunch."

"If I don't take good care of you, I'll never hear the end of it," Laurie said. "In case you didn't know, Mom's really worried about you."

"I realize that, but she doesn't need to

worry. I'm feeling fine right now." *Except for missing Luke,* she thought. *I don't know if I'll ever recover from that.*

Laurie patted Meredith's arm, the way Mom often did. "That's great, and we want to keep you feeling fine."

Meredith smiled. Laurie reminded her in many ways of their mother. She had the same blond hair and pale blue eyes. She even had Mom's light complexion and oval face. Meredith figured the way Laurie looked right now was probably how Mom must have looked when she was nineteen.

"Sure wish I could get the boppli's room painted," Meredith said, redirecting her thoughts. "There's so much left that needs to be done before the baby comes."

"I know, but with the help of your friends and family, it'll get done."

Meredith sighed. "I hate asking for help all the time, but now I feel like I have no other choice."

Laurie set her cup of hot chocolate on the coffee table, and turned to face Meredith. "You need to let others help. Remember, as Grandma Smucker always says: 'Next to the gift of Jesus

Christ, the greatest gifts in life are family and friends.'"

Laurie was right, but that didn't make it any easier to accept help. Meredith was about to suggest that they go to the kitchen to see about fixing their lunch, when she heard the *clip-clop* of horse's hooves coming up the driveway.

"Someone's here," Laurie said, jumping up from her chair. "Maybe it's Mom or Dad."

Meredith watched as her sister went to the door. Several minutes later, Laurie returned to the living room with Jonah at her side. He smiled and held a paper sack out to Meredith. "Your mamm asked me to bring these ginger cookies to you, and there are some primroses on the porch."

"Oh, you saw Mom today?"

He nodded. "I stopped by your folks' house to see how you were doing, and your mamm said you were here."

"That's right, and I'm happy to say that I'm doing much better now and was more than ready to come home."

"I'm glad to hear that, but you need to take it easy and not try to do too much," he warned.

Meredith stiffened. First Mom, then Laurie,

and now Jonah? Why did everyone think they needed to tell her what to do?

"Would you like me to plant the flowers for you?" Jonah asked. "Today's my day off, and I have nothing better to do."

"We'd appreciate that," Laurie said before Meredith could respond. "And when you're done, you can join us for lunch, and we'll have the ginger kichlin for dessert." She glanced quickly at Meredith. "Isn't that right, Sister?"

Meredith nodded. What else could she do? With Jonah offering to plant the flowers, she couldn't very well say no to him joining them for lunch.

"That sounds good," Jonah said with a grin. "But don't go to any trouble on my account."

"It'll just be soup and sandwiches, and I'll start fixing our lunch right now." Laurie flashed Jonah a wide smile and hurried from the room.

Meredith didn't know why, but she felt kind of awkward and shy around Jonah. She was relieved when he said he was going to plant the flowers and went out the door.

Rising from the sofa, she headed for the kitchen to see what she could do to help Laurie with lunch.

"What are you doing in here?" Laurie asked, turning from the stove, where she was stirring a kettle of leftover vegetable soup.

"I came to help."

Laurie shook her head. "I can manage just fine. Besides, you're supposed to be resting."

Meredith's fingers dug into the palms of her hands. "I'm not an invalid, Laurie, but if it would make you feel better, I'll sit at the table while I make the sandwiches."

"I guess that would be okay. Sorry if I seem so bossy." Laurie handed Meredith the sandwich fixings, along with some plates and a knife. "I'm just trying to do as Mom asked and take care of things so you can rest."

Meredith took a seat and relaxed against her chair. "I appreciate that, and I promise not to do anything strenuous."

"That's good to hear." Laurie stepped away from the stove and glanced out the window. "Looks like Jonah has gotten one bunch of primroses planted already. He sure is a nice man. Makes me wonder why he's not married."

Meredith shrugged. "I don't know. I guess he hasn't found the right woman yet."

"Jah, maybe so." Laurie remained at the

window a few more seconds, then returned to her job at the stove.

I wonder if my sister is interested in Jonah, Meredith thought. *I suppose the two of them might get together someday, but Laurie doesn't really seem like Jonah's type.* Meredith opened the bread wrapper and took out several slices. *But then, I guess that's really none of my business. I just need to concentrate on getting ready for the birth of my baby.*

CHAPTER 5

"This is sure a *gut middaagesse*. Danki for inviting me to stay for the meal," Jonah said after he'd eaten a few spoonfuls of soup.

Laurie smiled at him from across the table. "I'm glad you think the lunch is good. With the weather warming more every day, it won't be long before we'll want something cold to eat."

"That's probably true for most," Jonah agreed, "but I like soup just about any time of the year. It's a hearty meal that sticks with you. Least it does for me. And by the way, don't let this weather fool you. Winter can remind us that it's not letting go just yet. I know the wind isn't slowing up any."

Meredith sat quietly eating as her sister and Jonah continued chatting.

"Do you ever get tired of working on buggies?" Laurie asked, placing a sandwich on her plate, while looking at Jonah with an eager expression.

Jonah shook his head. "I like what I do, and since I've also started making other types of buggies that aren't for the Amish, it's created some new and interesting challenges for me."

Meredith stared at her half-eaten bowl of soup, barely listening to the conversation going on around her. She felt tired all of a sudden and really had no appetite. However, for the baby's sake, she needed to eat regular meals, so she forced herself to finish the soup and eat half a sandwich.

"You're awfully quiet," Jonah said, lightly touching Meredith's arm. "Am I boring you with all this talk about my job?"

Meredith jumped at his unexpected touch. "Uh, no. Guess I just don't have much to say." She quickly reached for a napkin and blotted her lips. "I'm feeling kind of tired, so if you two don't mind, I think I'll go back to the living room and rest awhile."

"Go right ahead," Laurie was quick to say. "Plenty of rest is what you need right now."

Wordlessly, Meredith cleared her dishes and placed them in the sink. She was almost to the kitchen door, when Jonah called, "Meredith, is there anything else you might need me to do?"

She turned, and was about to say no, when Laurie spoke up. "Actually, there is something. Meredith is planning to use one of the spare bedrooms upstairs for the boppli's room, and it needs to be painted."

Meredith's face heated as her lips tightened. *How could Laurie embarrass me like this?* She looked at Jonah and forced a smile. "I'm sorry my sister brought that up. I certainly don't expect you to do any painting. My daed will get it done whenever he finds the time. And if he can't do it, then. . ."

Jonah held up his hand. "I don't mind painting. In fact, I'd be happy to do it, and I have the time right now."

"That'd be great." Laurie smiled at Jonah. "Why don't we go upstairs, and I'll show you which room? The paint's sitting out, and the ladder's up there already, so everything's all set to go."

Jonah looked at Meredith, as though seeking her approval.

"It's fine with me, if you're sure," she said quietly. It was hard enough to accept help from her family and close friends, and it made her feel funny to have Jonah, whom she really didn't know that well anymore, here at the house doing chores for her—chores she'd once planned to do herself.

Jonah gave her a lopsided grin. "I'm definitely ready to begin."

"Before I forget," Meredith added, "danki for planting those flowers for me."

"You're welcome. The soil was good and wet from the rain we had earlier, so they were easy to put in the ground."

Meredith stood awkwardly, looking at the floor, unsure of what else to say. She was glad when Laurie turned to Jonah and said, "Okay then. I'll lead the way." She paused a moment and smiled at Meredith. "I'll do the dishes as soon as I show Jonah the room."

Meredith nodded and started for the living room. She was certain her sister was interested in Jonah. The whole time they'd been eating lunch, Laurie could hardly take her eyes off him, and the slight blush on Laurie's cheeks made it apparent that she felt attracted to him. Meredith wondered if Jonah noticed Laurie's interest. Could he be attracted to her, too? If so, Mom would be pleased, because she was always saying she wished Laurie had more of a social life.

But it's none of my business, Meredith reminded herself as she wandered over to the living-room window and looked out. Luke's horse was moving about in the corral. A lump formed in her throat. Seeing Socks there made her feel guilty for selling him, and worse than that, it caused her to think about Luke. If he hadn't been killed, he would have been painting their baby's room, not Jonah. If Luke were still alive, she wouldn't need her sister's help, either. If Luke were here, they'd be making plans for when the baby came and taking childbirth classes together at the midwife's clinic.

She closed her eyes and tried to imagine that Luke was right there. She could almost see him helping her paint the baby's room, going to childbirth classes with her, and holding their baby. It was so clear and real, it was nearly a shock when Laurie came down the stairs and announced that Jonah needed some rags.

Meredith quickly wiped away the tears that had crept from her eyes. "You'll find a box of *lumpe* in the utility room."

When Laurie left the room, Meredith moved away from the window and curled up on the sofa. *No amount of wishing will bring Luke back,* she told herself, squeezing her eyes tightly shut. *Dear, Lord, will it ever stop hurting so much?*

When Jonah left Meredith's house later that day, he was tired, sweaty, and speckled with beige paint. For once, the persistent breezes actually felt good after painting all afternoon in the stuffy room. Jonah hadn't wanted to make the upstairs too chilly for Meredith, so he'd opened the window in the room he'd painted, just a little, for ventilation. He would never have admitted it to Meredith, but painting walls was not really his thing. He was glad he'd been able to help her, though. She had seemed a bit hesitant at first, but when she'd seen the finished room she'd smiled and said he had done a good job and that she appreciated all his hard work.

Jonah planned to check on Meredith as often as he could, and if there were other things that needed to be done, he'd gladly do them. He just hoped she'd be willing to accept his help.

Jonah gripped the reins a bit tighter as Socks shook his head and started to trot. "Whoa there, steady boy. What's your rush, anyways?"

The horse had been in no hurry when they'd first left Meredith's place. In fact, Socks had balked like a stubborn mule when Jonah tried backing him away from the hitching rail. He figured the horse was familiar with his surroundings and didn't want to leave. Then, too, maybe Socks thought Luke was coming back. Either way, it had taken some coaxing to get the horse down the driveway and onto the main road, and now the unpredictable animal wanted to run at lightning speed. Of course, it hadn't helped when Meredith's dog started barking and running back and forth in his kennel.

Jonah felt the relentless wind rushing against his still-perspiring skin. A chill went through him, and he pulled his jacket tighter around his neck. March was the month when everyone celebrated spring's arrival, but it could be a real teaser. Jonah felt good whenever he could get outside and use all that pent-up energy he'd been storing through the winter to get something done. Then days later, it could be just the opposite, reminding him that winter was still hanging on and he'd have to wait a bit for more of those spring-fever days. It was always nice when the winds were behind them and April came rushing in.

One thing's for sure, Jonah thought. *This horse of mine will keep me on my toes. I'll have to remember not to let my guard down no matter where I am or what the weather is like.*

Jonah's thoughts went to Meredith again. He could tell she was struggling with depression over losing Luke. It was understandable, though. Who wouldn't be despondent after they'd lost a loved one—especially when they'd thought they had their whole future together? Jonah knew from seeing all that his sister Jean had gone through that grieving for a loved one was an ongoing process that required continued help and support. But Jean had made it through the rough times after losing Abe, so he felt sure that Meredith would, too. She just needed time to heal, and support from friends and family would surely help.

By the time Jonah turned his horse and buggy up the lane leading to his folks' house, he was exhausted. He'd had to fight for control of Socks almost the whole way. He'd just gotten Socks unhitched from the buggy when Herbie came running around the side of the house, barking and wagging his tail.

"Stay back!" Jonah shouted, but it was too late. The dog was already nipping at the horse's feet.

When Jonah loosened his grip slightly on the lead rope, Socks jerked free and took off after the dog.

Woof! Woof! Herbie raced around the yard, with Socks kicking his feet in the air, hot on the dog's tail. The next thing Jonah knew, Herbie took a flying leap and landed in a pile of manure on the side of the barn.

Jonah groaned. "Phew! What a *schtinke*!"

Mom rushed out of the house. "What's going on out here? What is all the commotion about?" Then she spotted Herbie yelping and rolling around in the grass. "Oh, no," she moaned, pointing to the dog. "How in the world did that happen?"

Jonah explained what had transpired and

ended with an apology. "Guess I should have kept a better hold on Socks. Just never expected Herbie to start nipping at him like that."

Mom's brows furrowed. "That gaul's been nothing but trouble since you bought him from Meredith. I know she needed the money and all, but you should have thought twice before bringing that unpredictable animal home."

"It wasn't the horse's fault that Herbie started nipping at his feet."

"That may be so," Mom replied, "but it is his fault that he chased after the dog, and now Herbie smells so bad he's going to need a bath."

"I'll do it," Jonah said, knowing it was probably the best way to get back in Mom's good graces. "Just give me a minute to get Socks put away in his stall, and then I'll fill one of the galvanized tubs for Herbie's bath."

"Just be sure you add some hot water to the tub. The weather's not warm enough to give the poor dog a cold-water bath." She studied Jonah a few seconds. "Looks like you could use a bath yourself. What have you been up to today?"

"I ran a few errands, and then I stopped by the Kings' place to see Meredith. But when I got there, I learned that she'd gone home and one of her sisters would be staying with her. So I went to Meredith's house to see how she was doing." Jonah motioned to the paint splatters on his arms. "Ended up planting some flowers and painting a room, but all in all, it was a pretty fair day." He looked at Herbie, still wallowing around the yard, and grimaced. "At least it was, until I came home."

Philadelphia

Susan's shift was just about done for the day, but before she left the floor, she wanted to check on her John Doe patient one last time. A few days ago, he'd taken a turn for the worse and had begun having seizures. The doctor had prescribed medication for the convulsions, and she hoped and prayed it was doing the job. This poor man had been through enough and deserved a chance to be well again.

"I'm going home now, Eddie, but I'll see you tomorrow," Susan said as she entered the patient's room and checked his vitals, ventilator, and feeding tube one last time. "Nurse Pamela will be here with you tonight, so you'll be in good hands."

No response. Not even the flutter of an eyelid.

Sometimes Susan felt foolish talking to her patient when he was in a coma, but there was a chance he could hear her, even if he wasn't able to respond. She couldn't imagine what it would be like to be trapped within one's own body. But then again, maybe the mind went someplace else—somewhere safe until the person eventually woke up.

Susan stopped at the foot of his bed. "Heavenly Father," she prayed out loud, "whoever this young man is, You must have a purpose for keeping him here on earth, so please touch his body as only You can."

CHAPTER 6

Bird-in-Hand

By the first of April, Meredith felt much better physically, and with Grandma Smucker helping her sometimes, she'd begun making head coverings to sell. She had been warned by the doctor, as well as her midwife, not to do anything strenuous and to let others help with the things she couldn't or shouldn't be doing. Meredith spent much of her time sewing on the coverings, and even though she sat to do it, she felt good to be actively doing something again. Sewing was relaxing, and it gave her plenty of time to plan and think about her new role as a mother.

Meredith also enjoyed going to the childbirth classes at the midwife's clinic a few miles up the road. Laurie went with her because she had agreed to be Meredith's coach. During the sessions, they learned the Bradley Method. Meredith was all in favor of using a more relaxed approach to childbirth, which this method emphasized. By practicing deep breathing and having Laurie's support as labor coach, Meredith would be able to deliver her baby without using drugs or going through surgery, unless she experienced a problem during labor. She also appreciated the emphasis on having a healthy baby and what she could do to eat right and stay in shape.

Meredith was glad she was no longer housebound and looked forward to going to the farmers' market with Alma in a week. Today was Friday, and Alma was baking bread, while Meredith sat at her Grandma King's old treadle sewing machine, making another head covering. Some women in their community used converted machines, run by a battery, but she preferred the old-fashioned kind. There was a sense of satisfaction that came from pumping her feet up and down to get the needle moving. Sitting at this older machine made Meredith think of all the things Grandma had made for her family over the years. Grandma and Grandpa King lived in a rural area of Kentucky, with Dad's brother Peter and his family, so Meredith didn't see them that often. Before they'd moved there four years ago, Grandma had given Meredith her old sewing machine, saying her fingers were stiff from arthritis, and she couldn't sew anymore.

Meredith glanced toward the kitchen door, listening to Alma hum while kneading her bread dough. Alma didn't have any children or grandchildren to pass things down to, but she'd been generous in sharing some personal items with those in their community. Just this morning, when Alma came over a few minutes before Laurie left for the market, she'd brought Meredith an old wooden cradle that had been hers when she was a baby. Meredith appreciated the gift but felt bad that Alma hadn't been able to use the heirloom for her own babies. If Luke were still here, their firstborn's cradle would have been made by him.

But she couldn't let her what-could-have-been thinking take over her life, and when thoughts like that entered her mind, she'd just have to let them go. She had to be positive.

This cradle would be special, too, because it was from Alma. She could feel Alma's love and encouragement, and appreciated all that the woman did to help out.

Meredith's gaze went to the cradle sitting in one corner of the living room. Tears sprang to her eyes. In just three short months her own baby would be lying in that cradle, and she could hardly wait. She hadn't told anyone, but she secretly hoped it would be a boy with his father's blond hair and beautiful turquoise eyes. Of course, if she had a little girl with strawberry-blond hair like hers, she would love her just as much. The fact that the child would be a part of Luke brought Meredith some measure of comfort.

"Are you ready to stop for lunch?" Alma asked when she ambled into the living room sometime later. "I've heated the leftover stew from last night, and we can have some fresh bread to go with it."

"That sounds *wunderbaar*." Meredith stopped sewing and patted her protruding stomach. "I didn't even realize I was *hungerich* until you mentioned food. That bread sure smells good. Now my belly won't stop growling."

Alma grinned and pushed a wisp of gray hair back under her covering. "I'll see you in the kitchen then, because just smelling the bread baking, along with that savory stew on the stove, has made my stomach rumble, too."

Meredith smiled as Alma headed back to the kitchen. She was glad Alma had remembered to turn her hearing aids on today so they could communicate easily. More times than not, Meredith ended up with a strained voice from talking loud enough for Alma to hear. But she never said anything about it, for Alma was such a sweet, caring person.

The slightly plump, rosy-cheeked woman was in her early seventies, and her cooking and baking skills made Meredith feel her own paled in comparison. But it wasn't Alma's cooking Meredith admired the most; it was her sweet, gentle spirit and knowledge of the scriptures. Some folks—both Amish and English—didn't read their Bibles often enough, and therefore didn't always know when God was speaking to them. Alma, on the other hand, read her Bible faithfully and liked to talk about some of the verses she'd memorized. This morning when she'd first arrived, she'd quoted Matthew 5:4

to Meredith and talked about how God blessed and comforted those who mourn, and how that comfort often comes from family and friends who surround the grieving one with their love and support.

I needed that reminder today, Meredith thought as she pushed her chair away from the sewing machine and stood. Even though at first she hadn't wanted Laurie or Alma to stay with her, now she was glad to have their help, as well as their company. She especially appreciated listening to Alma talk about when she was a girl and how the Lord had given her a heart for other people's children when she'd found out she couldn't have any of her own. Alma was a remarkable woman, who had not only learned to accept the fact that she was barren, but had also relied heavily on the Lord, as well as her friends, after her husband's sudden death.

Meredith started toward the kitchen, but stopped for a minute and closed her eyes. *Thank You, heavenly Father, for bringing Alma into my home, and for the knowledge that You know my pain and will see me through this time of grief.*

Philadelphia

"I can't wait to see the look on their faces when we surprise Grandma and Grandpa tonight," Anne told Susan as they ate lunch. It was one of those rare times when they had the same schedule and could actually meet in the hospital cafeteria at noon.

Susan smiled as she sprinkled a little salt on her hard-boiled egg. "It's not often we get to do anything special for them, so I hope everything works out as we've planned."

"I'm sure it will," Anne said in a confident tone, scraping the container of her tuna salad. "I mean, what could go wrong?"

"Nothing, I hope." Tonight was their grandparents' forty-fourth wedding anniversary, and Susan and Anne had planned a surprise dinner in their honor at Keya Graves, a lovely seafood and steakhouse in Darby. They'd invited Grandma and Grandpa's closest friends, and told their grandparents to meet them there at seven o'clock this evening. Grandma and Grandpa had no idea that family and friends would arrive half an hour early and be waiting to surprise them when the hostess ushered them into the restaurant's banquet room.

"I'm thrilled that everyone we invited is coming," Anne added. "Usually with an event like this, a few people can't make it."

"You're right, and it's an indication of how well Grandma and Grandpa are liked," Susan added. "Everything should be perfect, right down to the old-fashioned anniversary cake we ordered."

"Any change with your Eddie fellow?" Anne asked.

"He's stopped having seizures, so that's one positive thing."

Anne smiled and took a bite of her apple. "It sure is. Do you think he'll be moved to rehab soon?"

"I don't know. Guess it all depends on whether he continues to progress."

Deep lines formed across Anne's forehead as she slowly shook her head. "I wonder if we'll ever know who's responsible for that young man's injuries."

Susan shrugged. "I'm still hoping and

praying, but only the Lord knows what lies ahead for poor Eddie."

Bird-in-Hand

"I know Mom's not back from her dental appointment yet, but when she gets here, would you let her know that I might be a little late for supper?" Jonah asked his dad as they finished up their work in the buggy shop.

Dad's bushy eyebrows furrowed. "Are ya goin' someplace?"

"Thought I'd hitch up my horse and take a ride over to Meredith's house. I haven't seen her for a few days, and I'd like to know how she's doing and see if she needs my help with anything else."

Dad tapped his foot as he stared at Jonah. "You've been goin' over there a lot lately. Aren't ya worried about what others will say?"

Jonah tipped his head. "What is it you think they might say?"

Dad cleared his throat real loud. "Do I need to remind you that Meredith's a young widow, and she's expecting a boppli besides?"

A rush of heat spread across Jonah's face. "Exactly what are you saying, Dad?" he asked.

"I just feel you oughta be concerned about what others may think. Some folks could get the idea that you have it in mind to make Meredith your wife."

Oh, great, Jonah thought. *Now I'm in for one of Dad's long lectures. I'd better put an end to this before it gets started.*

"Look, Dad," Jonah said, talking slowly and deliberately, "I'm helping Meredith because she's a friend, and after seeing what Jean went through when she lost Abe, I want to do whatever I can to help Meredith during this difficult time. That's all there is to it, and I don't care what anyone thinks." Before Dad could say anything more, Jonah slapped his straw hat on his head and rushed out the door.

A short time later, after he'd washed up and changed his clothes, Jonah headed down the road with his horse and buggy. He didn't know if it was because Socks was getting used to him, or just pure luck, but for the first time since he'd acquired the horse, Socks was actually behaving himself.

Jonah looked out at the freshly planted fields and figured as long as they didn't get any flooding, the corn and other crops would do well with the spring rain they'd been having. The last couple of days had been rainy and raw, but the sun had come out around noon today, causing everything to smell clean and fresh. The harsh winds had finally died down, making room for milder days. Seeing the grass green up and the trees and flowers bloom, gave Jonah a sense of joy and anticipation for the future. He hoped Meredith sensed that, too, for she certainly needed the hope of spring—something positive to look forward to.

As Jonah approached Meredith's house, Socks picked up speed, and when he turned the horse up the driveway, Socks ran all the way to the barn.

Jonah chuckled. "This is home to you, isn't it, boy?"

Socks whinnied as if in response.

Woof! Woof! Fritz barked out a greeting from his kennel. As soon as Jonah had the horse secured to the hitching rail, he strode across the yard to greet the dog.

"You're smart, just like Herbie, aren't ya,

boy?" Jonah reached his hand through the wire fencing and stroked Fritz's silky head.

Plink! Plink! A few drops of water landed on his hand. He looked up and noticed that the canvas tarp, held up by four poles over part of Fritz's dog run, was full of rainwater.

"All that water needs to come off," Jonah said, giving Fritz another pat. "Otherwise the tarp might break, and you'll end up with a bath you probably don't want."

Fritz looked up at Jonah and whined. Did the animal understand what he'd said?

Jonah unlatched the gate and let Fritz out. "Go on now, boy! Go up to the house."

Fritz hesitated a minute, then tore across the yard and leaped onto the porch.

Jonah looked around for something he could use to drain the water from the tarp. He spotted a broken tree limb lying just outside the kennel, so he picked it up. Standing directly under the tarp, he gave it a good push. A quick burst of water rolled off one end, but most of it remained in the middle.

Jonah pushed against the tarp once more, this time jiggling the limb around a bit.

R-r-i-i-p! W-o-o-sh! The canvas tore down

the middle, and a blast of chilling water poured out on Jonah's head, drenching his shirt and trousers, and finding its way into his boots.

"Oh, great," Jonah moaned. "Now what have I done?"

CHAPTER 7

Meredith set her sewing aside and glanced at the clock on the wall above the fireplace. It was a quarter after six, and soon it would be time to eat supper. She was surprised Laurie wasn't back from the farmers' market yet. The market closed at five thirty, and Laurie's driver usually had her home by six.

Try not to worry, she told herself. *They probably got caught up in traffic, which is normal for a Friday evening.*

Meredith was about to head for the kitchen to see if Alma needed any help, when a knock sounded on the door. She hadn't heard a vehicle or horse and buggy come up the driveway, but then she'd been engrossed in her work.

Meredith opened the front door. Jonah stood there, soaking wet. Fritz sat beside him, perfectly dry. "*Ach*, Jonah, what happened?"

"I—I tried to get the water off the tarp co–covering Fritz's dog house," Jonah explained through chattering teeth. "And I–I'm afraid in my eagerness to do a good job, I ended up t–tearing a hole in the canvas, so all the w–water spilled out on me." Jonah leaned away from Meredith and shook water from his hair. "It's not that chilly outside today, but the water was c–cold as ice."

Meredith stifled a giggle. Poor Jonah looked so miserable, but he also looked funny with his thick, curly hair sticking out in all directions and water dripping down his face. "I'm so sorry that happened," she said. "You'd better come inside and get warm." Meredith hesitated a moment, then added, "My husband was about the same size as you, so you can borrow some of his clothes."

Jonah gave her a sheepish grin. "I appreciate that. If I t–tried to go home like this, I'd not only get the inside of my b–buggy all wet, but I'd probably lose my grip on the reins. My hands are almost numb."

When Meredith opened the door wider, Jonah stepped in and stood on the small braided entrance rug. "It's okay, pup," she said looking down at Fritz. "You can come in, too." She smiled as the dog went over and flopped down in his usual spot near her rocking chair. "If you'll wait right here, I'll go upstairs and get you some clothes," she said to Jonah. "And it looks like you'll need a towel as well."

Jonah, looking more than a little grateful as well as a bit embarrassed, nodded. While he waited in the entryway, Meredith went upstairs to get the clothes. She hadn't given away any of Luke's things, because she couldn't part with them, even though they'd go to good use if she gave them to the local thrift shop. Maybe someday she'd be ready to give his things up, but not yet. She wanted to save a few articles of clothing, anyway, to show their baby when he was old enough to be told about his father.

Meredith opened the dresser and took out a pair of Luke's black trousers and the pale blue shirt she had made for his last birthday. Just holding them made her tear up.

Out of impulse, she bent her head into the material of his shirt and inhaled deeply. It was freshly laundered, but she could still smell the fragrance of Luke. Or maybe it was just the idea of touching something Luke had worn that made her feel so gloomy all of a sudden.

Struggling to keep her emotions in check, Meredith went downstairs and handed the clothes to Jonah. "You can change in there," she said, pointing to the bathroom down the hall. "You'll find some towels in the closet behind the door."

Jonah hesitated a minute, looking at Meredith with obvious compassion. Did he know how hard it was for her to let him wear Luke's clothes?

"Go ahead. I'll wait for you in the living room," she said.

"Danki." Jonah went quietly down the hall.

Meredith returned to the living room, and as she seated herself in the rocking chair and reached down to pet Fritz's head, the baby kicked. The joy of feeling that movement drove her tears away, and she smiled, placing both hands against her stomach. It was so amazing, feeling life within her belly. Sometimes it felt light, like a butterfly fluttering around. Other times, such as now, she felt a good solid kick or two. If the baby turned out to be a boy, she might name him after his father. If it was a girl, she'd have to come up with a name she liked.

When Jonah returned to the living room a short time later, tears sprang to Meredith's eyes once again. Seeing him dressed in Luke's shirt and trousers was almost her undoing.

"I tossed my wet clothes out on the porch, and I'll bring your husband's clothes back tomorrow after work," Jonah said, shifting from one foot to the other. Did he feel as uneasy as she did right now?

"I'll get you a plastic sack." Meredith stood, but before she could take a step, Alma entered the room.

"Oh, it's you, Jonah. Thought I heard voices out here. Did you come to join us for supper?" Alma asked.

He shook his head. "Just dropped by to see how Meredith was doing and ask if she needed me to do anything."

Alma's gaze went to Meredith. "So, do you have anything for this nice young man to do?"

Meredith, feeling more flustered by the minute, could only shake her head. It was strange how she felt when Jonah was around.

Years ago, when they'd become friends in Florida, she was as comfortable with him as with any of her other friends. But now, for some reason, she felt somewhat uneasy around Jonah, and even a little guilty, wondering how others would feel about their friendship given that she was a widow.

"Well, since you're here, Jonah, and I have supper ready, I think you ought to join us," Alma practically insisted. "There's plenty to eat, and one more at the table won't make any difference."

Before Jonah could respond, the back door opened, and Laurie joined them.

"Hello, Jonah," she said, her lips curving into a wide smile. "I knew that was your horse and buggy out there because I recognized Socks. It's nice to see you again."

He nodded in response. "Same here."

There it is again, Meredith thought, walking into the kitchen to get Jonah a bag for his wet clothes. *That special look on Laurie's face whenever she sees Jonah. I wonder if I should talk to her about it—warn her that Jonah might already have a girlfriend in Ohio, or that she's being too forward. Or maybe it's best if I don't say anything. She might not appreciate it, and what if I'm wrong about things, and it's just my imagination?*

"Guess I'd better get going," Jonah said when Meredith came back, handing him the plastic sack.

He was almost out the door when Laurie hollered, "Aren't you gonna join us for supper?" She sniffed the air. "From that delicious aroma, I'm sure Alma's made something special."

"I appreciate the invite, but my mamm's probably holding supper for me right now, so I'd better go." Jonah gave a quick smile and hurried out the door.

Meredith turned to Laurie. "How come you're so late?"

Laurie's face flamed. "What's the matter, Meredith, don't you trust me?"

"Of course I do," Meredith replied. "Why would you even ask such a question?"

"Well, you looked upset when you asked why I was late, and I thought maybe. . ."

Meredith held up her hand. "I was only concerned because you're not usually late. And since this is Friday night, when traffic is usually worse, I couldn't help but worry."

"Sorry about that, but I stayed awhile to

help one of the other vendors put some things away in his booth. And you're right—there was a lot of traffic."

"That's okay, you're here now, so let's eat," Alma said, motioning to the kitchen.

Meredith didn't know why, but she had a funny feeling her sister wasn't being completely honest. Of course, she saw no reason for Laurie to lie, so she was probably imagining that, as well.

Ronks

Sitting around the kitchen table with her family that evening, Luann smiled at her youngest son, Owen, as he chomped away on a juicy drumstick. Grandma Smucker had made fried chicken for supper, and everyone seemed to be enjoying it.

"This chicken is *appenditlich*, Grandma," eight-year-old Arlene said, licking her fingers.

Luann's mother smiled. "I'm glad you think it's delicious."

Luann's sixteen-year-old daughter, Kendra, wrinkled her nose and glared at Arlene. "It's not polite to lick your fingers, Sister."

"Maybe not," Luann's husband, Philip, put in, "but this chicken is finger-lickin' good." He swiped his tongue over his fingers and grinned at Luann's mother, who gave him a wide smile in return.

"Not to change the subject or anything," Luann said, "but Meredith's birthday is coming up in two weeks, so I think it would be nice if we did something special to celebrate."

"That's a good idea." Nina, who was fourteen, nodded her head. "That will let Meredith know how much we love her."

"I don't think Meredith will be up to a big party," Grandma said. "Maybe a nice, small family gathering is all that she needs."

"Just a little celebration among us," Luann agreed. "I can make her favorite cake and decorate it the way I used to when she was little. I'll even make it a three-tiered cake and use the pretty glass cake dish you used for my birthday when I was growing up," she added, looking at her mother.

"That all sounds good to me—especially the cake," Philip said with a wink.

"Let's make it a surprise, though, because if

we tell Meredith we want to have a get-together for her birthday, she'll probably say not to bother or that she doesn't feel like celebrating this year," Luann said. "We'll tell Laurie and Alma about it, of course. Maybe Alma can take Meredith someplace that afternoon, and while they're gone, I'll go over to Meredith's house and get things ready. I'll make sure to tell Alma not to bring Meredith home until six o'clock. By then, we'll all be there, ready to surprise Meredith when they get back."

"What about our horses and buggies?" Stanley asked as he pulled the fried coating from his piece of chicken and ate that first. "Won't Meredith see 'em out in the yard and know we're there?"

"We can put the horses in the barn and hide the buggies around back," Philip responded.

Stanley grinned. "That's a good idea, Dad."

"I think so, too, and I'm gonna make Meredith a pretty birthday card with birds on it." Arlene grinned. "Meredith likes feeding the birds in her yard."

"Should we invite Luke's folks, as well as Meredith's friend Dorine and her family, too?" Luann asked Philip.

He nodded. "I think they'd feel left out if we didn't."

"All right then, I'll start working out the details tomorrow morning." Luann looked at her mother. "Would you like to help me plan things, Mom?"

A big smile formed on the elderly woman's face. "Of course I would."

Darby

"This is really a nice place," Susan said as she and Anne entered the restaurant. Several of Grandma and Grandpa's closest friends had already arrived, and they'd been taken to the banquet room, where tables had been set up with a few anniversary decorations. The cake had been safely delivered; the guests were all there; all they needed now was Grandma and Grandpa.

While everyone visited, Susan kept checking her watch. Forty minutes later, when they still hadn't arrived, Susan turned to Anne and said, "Grandma and Grandpa should have been here by now. Think I'd better give them a call."

"That's a good idea," Anne agreed. "Maybe we shouldn't order our meals until they get here."

Susan pulled out her cell phone and called Grandma's cell number. All she got was her voice mail. She left a message, then dialed the home number, but only got the answering machine there. The later it got, the more she worried. *Now where could they be? The weather's not bad or anything. It just doesn't make sense.*

"Do you think they forgot?" Susan asked Anne.

Anne shrugged. "They could have, I guess. Either that or they got lost, which would make no sense since the restaurant isn't all that far from their home." She motioned to one of the tables where several elderly couples sat. "It's getting late, and I'm sure everyone's hungry, so I think we should go ahead and let these good people order their meals. If Grandpa and Grandma haven't arrived by the time everyone's done eating, we'll head for home and hope that they're there."

"Okay," Susan agreed. "I pray that Grandma and Grandpa are all right.

Upper Darby, Pennsylvania

"I don't see any sign of Susan or Anne," Norma Bailey said to her husband, Henry, when they entered the Italian restaurant where they were supposed to meet their granddaughters.

"They probably got waylaid at the hospital," Henry said. "You know how that can be when things get busy."

Norma nodded as she took her seat at the table their hostess had shown them. "I think I'll give the girls a call and let them know we're here." She reached into her purse for her cell phone. "Oh, oh."

"What's wrong?"

"No cell phone. I must have left it at home."

Henry frowned. "Never did have much use for those little gadgets. They're so small, no wonder you forgot it. Probably wouldn't have seen it if it'd been right under your nose."

She laughed and elbowed his arm. "Are you saying my eyesight is failing?"

"No, I'm saying most of those cell phones

are way too small." He glanced at his watch. "Do you think maybe the reason the girls aren't here is because we have the wrong night?"

"I suppose that's possible, but I'm almost certain they said they'd meet us here tonight." Norma glanced across the room. "Say, isn't that Mary and Ben Hagen, the new couple from church?"

Henry's gaze followed hers. "I believe it is."

"Maybe we should ask them to join us."

His eyebrows furrowed. "What about Susan and Anne?"

"What about them?"

"Won't they be upset when they get here and see that we've invited someone to join our little party?"

Norma shook her head. "Our granddaughters are both very social. I'm sure they won't mind a few extra people at our table. Besides, we should make the Hagens feel welcome, so why don't you go over there and invite them to join us?"

Henry's eyebrows furrowed. "Why me? It was your idea, Norma."

She clicked her tongue. "All right then, I'll invite them."

A few minutes later, Norma returned with Mary and Ben. They all ordered their meals and got busy talking. When the couple mentioned that their twenty-seven-year-old grandson, Brian, who was single, would be visiting during the summer, Norma perked right up, saying they'd have to make sure that he met Susan, who was close to his age.

When their meal was over, the Baileys decided to go home. Susan and Anne were obviously not coming.

When they entered their house sometime later, Norma was surprised to discover their granddaughters sitting in the kitchen with an anniversary cake.

"Where have you been?" Susan asked, jumping up from the table. "We've been crazy with worry about you."

"That's right," Anne agreed. "How come you didn't meet us at the restaurant?"

Henry's eyebrows pulled together. "What do you mean? We were there. Where were you two girls?"

"We were there with some of your good friends waiting for you." Susan tipped her head and looked at Henry with a peculiar expression.

"What restaurant did you and Grandma go to?"

"Pica's Italian Restaurant in Upper Darby. Isn't that where we were supposed to meet?"

"No, it was Keya Graves, the seafood and steakhouse here in Darby." Susan looked at Anne, and they both burst out laughing. When they finally quit, Susan explained that she'd tried to call but had only gotten voice mail and that they'd ended up eating at the restaurant with Grandma and Grandpa's friends and had brought the cake home.

Norma chuckled and then told the girls how they'd met Mary and Ben and eaten supper with them.

Henry pointed to the cake. "Well, we may not have celebrated our anniversary dinner with you two, but we can sure eat this tasty-looking cake right now."

"Good idea." Susan jumped up and got out the plates, forks, and napkins, then cut the cake.

"This tastes just like the buttermilk cake we had on our wedding day." Norma smiled at the girls after she'd taken her first bite.

"It is," Anne said. "We found a bakery that makes vintage cakes, and couldn't believe it when we described your wedding cake and were told that they could make one just like it."

As they ate, they visited and laughed some more about the crazy evening and how it had turned out. Although not together, at least they'd all had a good meal.

"It's good to see you laughing," Norma said, patting Susan's arm. "You've been much too serious lately—probably due to all the stresses at work and worrying about your John Doe patient."

Susan smiled as she started clearing the dishes. "You're right, and this has been a fun evening, even if you didn't get to celebrate your anniversary with all your closest friends."

"We celebrated with our family," Norma said, "and that's what's important. But I'm sure we're going to be in for a lot of ribbing when we see some of those friends at church on Sunday."

"Especially when they find out we went to the wrong restaurant." Henry released a noisy yawn and stood. "Guess I'd better head for bed."

"Me, too," Norma agreed, rising to her feet. "It's been a long day and, I might add, an exciting evening."

"Before you leave the kitchen, there's something I wanted to say," Anne spoke up as she got the sponge to wipe a few crumbs off the table.

"What's that?" Henry asked, turning around.

"I wanted to remind you that Susan and I will be going to Lancaster County on Saturday, and you're more than welcome to join us."

"That's nice of you," Norma said, "but your grandpa and I already have plans."

He looked at her and quirked an eyebrow. "We do?"

She nodded. "We're getting together with Mary and Ben, remember?" She placed her hand on Susan's shoulder. "You two should go and have fun. If your grandpa and I went along, we'd only slow you down."

"I don't think so, Grandma," Susan said, giving Norma a hug. "But if you've made other plans, we understand."

"Well, good night then." Norma was glad Henry hadn't mentioned anything about Mary and Ben's grandson, because that would probably put Susan on the defensive. Norma had tried playing matchmaker with both Susan and Anne a few times, and it hadn't been well received.

Maybe I won't have to play matchmaker, she told herself. *I'll just keep praying that God will bring the right men into my granddaughters' lives. After all, He knows better than I do who Susan and Anne both need, and if it's meant to happen, it will be in His time.*

Chapter 8

Bird-in-Hand

"This day is turning out to be so much fun," Anne said to Susan as they pulled into the parking lot at the farmers' market on Saturday afternoon.

"Oh, I know," Susan agreed. "The homemade rootbeer and soft pretzel we had at that roadside stand awhile ago were sure good. I'm glad we bought a gallon of rootbeer to take home so Grandma and Grandpa can enjoy it, too."

"Yes, and it's a good thing you thought to bring the cooler along." Anne parked the car and turned off the ignition. "Maybe we'll find some other tasty morsels inside the market."

Susan chuckled. "If we eat anything else,

we'll probably be too full for supper."

"I don't care if I am," Anne said. "I've waited a long time for this trip, and I'm going to enjoy every minute of it—including the food. By the way, Susan, did I mention how much I like that cute pink blouse you're wearing today?"

"Glad you like it. On a whim, I stopped at the clothing store near the hospital the other day and found this on the bargain table." Susan held the market door open. "Now let's go see what we can find to eat!"

When they entered the building, Susan inhaled deeply, enjoying the delicious aromas coming from the various food vendors. At a booth near the door stood a man making fried corn fritters. The smell of coffee brewing was in the air, as well as the sweet aroma of baked goods coming from the stand across the aisle. From where she stood, Susan could see they had whoopie pies, apple fritters, homemade bread, cookies, and an assortment of delicious-looking pies. It would be hard to get past that booth without taking something home for dessert.

Susan glanced in one direction and then another, unable to take everything in. All the seats were filled in the eating area, and she noticed several people enjoying sandwiches and hot dogs.

"Let's start over here," Anne suggested, pointing to her right.

As they walked up and down the aisles, they stopped to sample some pickled vegetables, then moved on to taste a few homemade pretzels and chips with several dipping sauces.

"Look at this," Susan exclaimed as they approached a stand with unique wooden art. "Imagine taking an old shutter and turning it into something that beautiful."

"The artist must be very talented." Anne ran her hand over the smooth piece of shutter that had a deer scene carved into the wood. "I wonder if Grandpa would like something like this to hang on the living-room wall."

"I think he might. We'll get it for him before we leave," Susan said. "It'll make a nice belated anniversary gift to surprise him with."

"I'm thirsty now," Anne said as they continued browsing. She pointed to a vendor selling freshly squeezed lemonade. "Let's get something to drink."

Susan followed Anne over to the stand, and as they stood drinking their lemonade, she noticed a young, blond-haired Amish woman across the aisle selling faceless Amish dolls. "I think I'll go over there and see how much those dolls cost," she told Anne.

"Seriously? Are you thinking of buying one?"

Susan nodded. "I've always been fascinated with the Amish culture, and a doll like that would look cute on my bed."

"I'm fascinated, too, but I think I may buy a quilted wall hanging or table runner to give Grandma," Anne said. "We might find something else for Grandpa before we're done, as well."

Susan smiled. "Since the party we planned for them didn't work out, the least we can do is get each of them something nice."

"I think so, too," Anne agreed.

"I wonder if Grandpa would like one of those straw hats they're selling over there?" Susan pointed in the direction of the hats. "He could wear it when he's working in the yard, and it'll keep the sun off his head."

"That's a good idea. Let's get that for Grandpa, too," Anne said with a nod.

When they approached the stand where the Amish dolls were being sold, the young woman looked up at them and smiled. "Can I help you with something?"

"Yes, I'd like to know the price of your faceless dolls," Susan said.

"The smaller ones are thirty dollars, and the larger dolls are forty dollars."

"I think I'd like one of the larger dolls." Susan looked at Anne. "Should I get one with blond, brown, or auburn hair?"

Anne touched Susan's straight bob. "Well, since you're a brunette, why don't you get a doll with brown hair?"

Susan pursed her lips as she studied the dolls on display. "Come to think of it, I may get a boy doll and a girl doll—both with blond hair like Eddie's."

A crease formed across Anne's nose as she frowned. "This is our day off, and you're not supposed to be thinking about your patients."

"I know, but seeing the color of these dolls' hair made me think of him, that's all." She picked up one of the girl dolls and studied the detail of its clothes—a dark blue dress, white apron, and a little white cap. On the back of its cloth body was a tag that read: *Handmade by Laurie King.*

Susan smiled at the Amish woman. "Is your name Laurie? Did you make these dolls?"

"Jah. I mean, yes," Laurie replied. "I enjoy sewing, and I've been making dolls like these since I was fifteen."

"You don't look much more than that now," Anne interjected.

A pink blush erupted on the young woman's cheeks. "I'm nineteen," she said, dropping her gaze to the dolls.

"You do a nice job of sewing, and as soon as I make up my mind, I'm definitely going to buy at least one."

"It feels good to be here at the market," Meredith said as she and Alma walked past Groff's candy stand, where delectable-looking fudge, peanut brittle, nuts, and dried fruits beckoned people. "I just wish we'd gotten here a bit sooner, because everything will close down in an hour or so."

"I know, but I think we still have plenty of time to see what we want." Alma made a sweeping gesture of the booths nearby. "Even though there are bigger farmers' markets in the area, I like coming here because it's close to my home, and it's a much smaller market than some."

"That's true," Meredith agreed. "The Green Dragon and Roots Markets are a lot larger, but it's really hard to see everything; although I have enjoyed visiting those markets many times before."

They strolled past several other stands, and as they approached Sue's Sandwich Shoppe, Meredith halted. "Should we get some subs to take home for supper? That way we won't have to cook anything tonight."

"Uh. . .I'm not really in the mood for a sub sandwich."

"How about some other kind of sandwich or a pretzel dog?"

Alma shook her head. "You need a more substantial meal than that." She slipped her arm around Meredith's waist. "I'll fix us a hearty meal as soon as we get home."

Meredith didn't argue. If there was one thing she'd learned about Alma, it was that once she'd made her mind up about something, there was no changing it. And the truth was, her home-cooked meals were delicious, so

Meredith figured whatever Alma fixed would be a treat.

"If you're really hungry and can't wait for supper, why don't we snack on a few samples?" Alma suggested.

"Okay." Meredith led the way to her dad's stand, where he sold kettle corn. They visited with him awhile and tasted a few of the little cups he had setting out for people to try.

"Your kettle corn is as good as ever," Meredith said, leaning on the edge of his table.

"I've always enjoyed making it, and it sells really fast. Especially today, with the good crowd that's here." He grinned at Meredith. "By the way. . .*hallich gebottsdaag.* I heard you were coming here to celebrate your birthday."

She smiled and motioned to Alma. "It was her idea."

"And a good one it is," he said, winking at Alma.

Several people came up to Dad's stand then, so Meredith told him goodbye.

"Your mamm and I will see you tomorrow at church," Dad called as Meredith and Alma moved on.

Their next stop was the Kitchen Kettle

Village booth, where they sampled some pepper jam and chow-chow. Eating the chow-chow made Meredith think of Luke, because his mother made it often and Luke had always said that no one could make chow-chow quite like his mom.

Knowing she needed to focus on something else, Meredith suggested they go over to Laurie's stand and see how she was doing. When they arrived, she saw two young English women talking to Laurie, and one of them was buying two blond-haired dolls—a boy and a girl. Even the sight of the dolls caused Meredith to think about Luke, as their hair color was almost the same as his.

I've got to stop doing this, she told herself. *I can't dwell on how much I miss Luke every time I see something that reminds me of him.*

As Meredith and Alma stepped up to Laurie's table, she heard the English woman who wore blue jeans and a pink blouse say something about being a nurse. Then the other woman, also wearing jeans with a matching jacket, turned to Meredith and smiled. "These are beautiful dolls, aren't they?"

Meredith nodded. "My sister makes them."

"Oh, so Laurie King is your sister?"

"That's right." Meredith nodded as she smiled at Laurie.

"I'm glad you're here," Laurie said. "Could you and Alma give me a ride home?"

"We can, but I thought your driver would be picking you up."

"I'll explain in a few minutes," Laurie said. "I just need to make change for this customer and put her dolls in a box." Her forehead wrinkled as she studied Meredith. "You look tired. Why don't you take a seat behind my stand, and we can talk as soon as I'm done."

Meredith really wasn't that tired, but she quietly slipped behind the table and took a seat in one of the folding chairs. She figured Alma would do the same. Instead, Alma started up a conversation with the dark-haired women, who seemed to be full of questions about the Amish way of life. Finally, they thanked Laurie for the dolls and went on their way.

Meredith figured Laurie would say what was on her mind. Instead, she leaned across the table and whispered something to Alma.

"What are you two talking about?" Meredith asked, rising from her seat.

"Just discussing what we'll have for supper," Alma said, looking red-faced and a little flustered.

Meredith's lips compressed. She had a feeling there was more going on than just a discussion about what they'd be having for supper. Were they planning some kind of a birthday surprise behind her back? Meredith had thought Mom would invite her to their place for supper tonight, but she hadn't heard a word from Mom since earlier this week. It made her more than a little suspicious.

"Could you please hurry and get the dining-room table set?" Luann asked her daughter Kendra as they scurried around Meredith's kitchen, getting the final preparations for supper finished.

"Sure, Mom." Kendra removed a stack of plates from the cupboard and took them to the other room.

"I'm glad your daed could close up his stand and come home early to help out," Luann mentioned. "He's going to take care of hiding the horses and buggies when the Yoders and Luke's folks arrive."

"I heard Dad say that he sold out of kettle corn early today, so it was a good reason for him to leave the market before closing time," Kendra put in.

"He also told me that Meredith and Alma stopped by his booth, but he was able to sneak out soon after they headed to Laurie's stand." Luann chuckled as she gently stirred the fresh fruit salad. "So far, everything is working out." She smiled at her mother, who sat at the kitchen table making a tossed green salad. "When I stopped by the farmers' market this morning to see Laurie, she said she and Alma had planned it so that Alma and Meredith would go to the market this afternoon, and then she would ask them for a ride home."

"I think Meredith will be very surprised," her mother said. Then she grinned at Arlene, Katie, and Owen as they stood staring at the beautiful cake she'd decorated earlier. "You kids can look at the cake, but don't touch."

"I won't," Arlene said with a quick shake of her head. "And I'll make sure my little bruder and schweschder don't touch it, neither."

Luann smiled. Arlene always did like bossing the two younger ones around. "I hope Laurie doesn't give our surprise party away," she said. "She's never been very good at keeping secrets, you know."

"I'm sure it'll all work out," her mother said in a positive tone.

Luann glanced nervously out the window. "I wonder where Seth, Dorine, and Luke's folks are? I figured they'd be here by now."

"Don't you start fretting. I'm sure everything will work out fine."

"I just want everything to be perfect. Meredith deserves to have a happy time tonight."

"You're right. She does." Luann's mother went to the refrigerator to get a bottle of salad dressing. She'd no more than returned to the table when Luann heard the rumble of buggy wheels outside. She glanced out the window again and smiled. "Oh good, Sadie and Elam are here, and I see the Yoders' buggy coming in right behind them."

"I brought a potato salad and some deviled eggs," Sadie said when she and Dorine entered the house with Dorine's two little ones in tow. "Elam and Seth are putting the horses in the barn, and Philip's hiding the buggies."

Dorine glanced around. "Meredith's not here yet, I hope."

Luann shook her head. "I expect she, Alma, and Laurie will arrive soon, though."

The women visited while they continued with the supper preparations, and a few minutes after the men came in, another horse and buggy rumbled up the driveway.

"It's Meredith," Philip announced, peering out the window. "If we're gonna surprise her, then we'd better all hide."

Meredith was a little disappointed when she guided her horse up to the hitching rail and didn't see any other buggies parked in the yard. Maybe she'd been wrong about her family planning a party for her.

"I'll put the horse away," Laurie was quick to say. "Just wait right here in the buggy until I get done."

"Now why would I do that? I'm perfectly capable of putting Taffy away in her stall." Meredith started to get out, but Alma, who sat in the backseat of the buggy, put her hand on Meredith's shoulder and said, "We did a lot of walking this afternoon, and I'm sure you're tired, so why not let your sister put the horse away?"

"Okay," Meredith relented, "but there's no reason for us to wait here until she's done. We should go in the house and get supper started."

Laurie had already led Taffy to the barn, but Alma just sat there, staring straight ahead.

"Alma, did you hear what I said?" Meredith questioned.

Alma tipped her head. "What was that?"

"We should go inside and fix something to eat."

"Did you say something about your feet?"

Meredith shook her head. "I said, eat, not feet. Alma, are your hearing aids turned on?"

Again, Alma said nothing.

Feeling a little perplexed, Meredith climbed down from the buggy and extended her hand to Alma. A few moments ago, Alma seemed to hear what she'd said, and now suddenly she couldn't? What was going on here anyway?

"I'm not so old that I can't get out of the

buggy by myself," Alma said. "It just takes me a little longer than some."

A little longer? Meredith thought. She'd never seen anyone be so slow about getting out of a buggy. At least Alma seemed to be hearing better again.

By the time Alma had finally climbed down, Laurie came out of the barn. "I'm sure hungerich," she said. "Let's get up to the house so we can fix something to eat."

"What about the buggy?" Meredith questioned. "It needs to be put in the buggy shed."

"I'll do it after supper." Laurie stepped between Meredith and Alma, placing her hands in the crook of their arms.

As they walked slowly to the house, Meredith wondered once again if something might be amiss. She opened the door and entered the house.

"Surprise! Hallich gebottsdaag, Meredith!" hollered a chorus of voices.

Tears welled in Meredith's eyes. It felt good to know her family loved her so much, and it would be a lot easier to put on a happy face this evening because they were here. But her heart still ached, for she missed Luke and wished he were also here to help celebrate her birthday. Somehow, she must learn to accept her loss, because no matter how much she wanted it, Luke wasn't coming back.

Meredith looked at each of her family members, as well as Alma, Sadie, Elam, Dorine, Seth, and their children. She couldn't have felt more loved and knew without a doubt how very blessed she was.

Philadelphia

Voices. . .Voices. . . Somewhere in a faraway place there were voices. What were they saying? Were they talking about him? Were they talking to him?

I feel like I'm suffocating and the darkness is swallowing me up. I need to open my eyes. I want to wake up.

Someone touched his arm. More voices—something about his blood pressure and pulse. He winced, feeling pain radiating from different parts of his body.

Pulling from somewhere deep inside, the man willed his eyes to open. He squinted against the bright light invading his senses and tried to focus on the faces before him. Who were these people, and why were they staring at him? He stared back, blinking several times, trying to make his eyes focus. A woman with blond hair smiled at him.

"Look, Doctor," she said, turning to the man who stood beside her. "I think our John Doe is finally awake."

About the Author

New York Times bestselling author, Wanda E. Brunstetter became fascinated with the Amish way of life when she first visited her husband's Mennonite relatives living in Pennsylvania. Wanda and her husband, Richard, live in Washington State but take every opportunity to visit Amish settlements throughout the States, where they have several Amish friends. Wanda and her husband have two grown children and six grandchildren. In her spare time, Wanda enjoys photography, ventriloquism, gardening, beachcombing, stamping, and having fun with her family.

To contact Wanda and to learn about her other books, visit Wanda's website at www.wandabrunstetter.com.

A Lancaster County Saga

THE STORY OF THE DISCOVERY CONTINUES WITH...

The Discovery: Part 4 – The Pieces of Summer
In *The Pieces of Summer*, part four of *New York Times* Bestselling author, Wanda E. Brunsetter's The Discovery—A Lancaster County Saga, it's only been a few months since Meredith Stoltzfus lost her husband, Luke, and deep down, she feels uncomfortable when Jonah Miller comes by often, so willing to help her with things around the house. Meanwhile, as a young, nameless man heals and regains strength in his body, his mind grasps at every image that flits across his memory, desperately trying to recall his former life. . . .

DON'T MISS A SINGLE BOOK IN THIS EXCLUSIVE 6-BOOK SERIAL NOVEL

The Discovery: Part 1 – *Goodbye to Yesterday*

The Discovery: Part 2 – *The Silence of Winter*

The Discovery: Part 3 – *The Hope of Spring*

The Discovery: Part 4 – *The Pieces of Summer*

The Discovery: Part 5 – *A Revelation in Autumn*

The Discovery: Part 6 – *A Vow for Always*

AVAILABLE AT YOUR FAVORITE BOOKSTORE

Other books by Wanda E. Brunstetter

Adult Fiction

The Half-Stitched Amish Quilting Club

Kentucky Brothers Series
The Journey
The Healing
The Struggle

Brides of Lehigh Canal Series
Kelly's Chance
Betsy's Return
Sarah's Choice

Indiana Cousins Series
A Cousin's Promise
A Cousin's Prayer
A Cousin's Challenge

Sisters of Holmes County Series
A Sister's Secret
A Sister's Test
A Sister's Hope

Brides of Webster County Series
Going Home
Dear to Me
On Her Own
Allison's Journey

Daughters of Lancaster County Series
The Storekeeper's Daughter
The Quilter's Daughter
The Bishop's Daughter

BRIDES OF LANCASTER COUNTY SERIES
A Merry Heart
Looking for a Miracle
Plain and Fancy
The Hope Chest

Amish White Christmas Pie

Lydia's Charm

Love Finds a Home
Love Finds a Way

Children's Fiction

DOUBLE TROUBLE
What a Pair!
Bumpy Ride Ahead

RACHEL YODER—ALWAYS TROUBLE SOMEWHERE SERIES

The Wisdom of Solomon

Nonfiction

Wanda E. Brunstetter's Amish Friends Cookbook
Wanda E. Brunstetter's Amish Friends Cookbook Vol. 2
The Simple Life
A Celebration of the Simple Life